W9-ATV-452

THE
PROSPECT

THE PROSPECT

Jason *Glaser*

MINNEAPOLIS

Text copyright © 2012 by Lerner Publishing Group, Inc.

All rights reserved. International copyright secured. No part of this book may be reproduced, stored in a retrieval system, or transmitted in any form or by any means—electronic, mechanical, photocopying, recording, or otherwise—without the prior written permission of Lerner Publishing Group, Inc., except for the inclusion of brief quotations in an acknowledged review.

Darby Creek
A division of Lerner Publishing Group, Inc.
241 First Avenue North
Minneapolis, MN 55401 U.S.A.

Website address: www.lernerbooks.com

The images in this book are used with the permission of:
© Kelpfish/Dreamstime.com, p. 109; © iStockphoto.com/Jill Fromer, p. 112 (banner background); © iStockphoto.com/ Naphtalina, pp. 112, 113, 114 (brick wall background). Front Cover: © Erik Isakson/CORBIS. Back Cover: © Kelpfish/Dreamstime.com.

Main body text set in Janson Text 12/17.5.
Typeface provided by Adobe Systems.

Glaser, Jason.
    The prospect / by Jason Glaser.
        p.   cm. — (Travel team)
    ISBN 978-0-7613-8325-3 (lib. bdg. : alk. paper)
    1. Baseball—Fiction.] I. Title.
PZ7.G480465Pr 2012
[Fic]—dc23   2011025984

Manufactured in the United States of America
1—BP—12/31/11

DEDICATED TO THE MEMORY OF
CORPORAL ANDREW WILFAHRT

"The way a team plays as a whole determines its success. You may have the greatest bunch of individual stars in the world, but if they don't play together, the club won't be worth a dime."

—BABE RUTH

CHAPTER 1

Nick Cosimo couldn't remember the last time catching a baseball in the web of his glove felt familiar. Had it ever? He pulled the ball out of the leather and gave it an easy lob over to his Las Vegas Roadrunners teammate and pitcher Shotaro Mori. Shotaro slung back a faster one. Nick concentrated to draw it into the soft pouch above his thumb and to curl his fingers closed.

Nick's well-worn catcher's mitt sat under

the bench, slumped like it was pouting. Coach Harris was big on his players keeping well-rounded baseball skills and not specializing too much too soon. It was too late for Nick, though. He would always be a catcher. Anything less than a soft *poomph* in the middle of the mitt would always sound and feel wrong.

"Did you hear about Dylan Johnson going upper third?" Shotaro asked as he threw another.

"*Everybody* knows about that," Nick called back. "It's everywhere."

"To the Yankees, man. The New York Yankees!" Shotaro's eyes seemed to glaze over, perhaps with images of himself in a Yankee uniform. His next throw was off target. Nick ran in a few steps to make the catch.

Nick snorted. "More like the Staten Island Yankees. Triple-A if he's lucky."

"I bet he makes the club in two or three years," Gus Toomey chimed in. He and Kurt Kinnard were also warming up their arms nearby. "I played on a team with Johnson a couple years ago. I don't think he struck out more than a dozen times the whole season."

"He's not so great," Kurt argued. "I could sit him down. Wasn't he projected for the second round?"

Nick remembered when Dylan first announced he was going in the draft. Several papers said he wouldn't go any higher than the fifth round. He was coming right out of high school, after all.

By now, they'd all stopped throwing the ball. Shotaro laughed. "Big talk, Kurt. How high do you think you're going in the draft?"

A big grin spread across Kurt's face—the same one he had just before he got you chasing his backwards breaking pitch. "First round's a given. I'm shooting for number one overall. Pitchers almost always go first overall."

Nick scrunched up his nose and peered back into the vast amounts of baseball trivia stored in his head. "Actually, pitchers have only been taken first fourteen times over the last sixty years. Less than twenty-five percent."

Kurt pointed to himself with his mitt. "Well, I'm gonna be number fifteen."

Gus crossed his arms. "You're going to have to wait for the year after me, then. Unless you're not going to college first."

The sharp shriek of a whistle made them all jump. Coach Harris loomed like a ghost behind them.

"You're all going back to the locker room if you don't start practicing for tomorrow's game," he yelled. "I sent you out here to warm up, and I haven't seen one throw out of you clowns in the last five minutes!"

The players quickly separated and once again started firing off throws.

"And, don't be getting your hopes up too high," Coach Harris continued. "I've coached hundreds of kids and seen maybe a couple get drafted.

"If you're going to stand out, you gotta be special. Something different, something better."

Then I'll get better, Nick thought to himself. *Me and different get along fine already.*

. . .

To Nick, it seemed like the strike zone had gone on a diet as he crouched behind the plate. Nick watched another pitch hum in over the outside corner, only to hear the umpire call out a half-hearted "Ball." The hometown crowd loudly booed the call. Traveling teams like the Roadrunners rarely had anything approaching a home-field advantage, but the locally run Las Vegas Invitational for U17 teams allowed hundreds of Roadrunner family members, supporters, and financial backers to crowd the stands. It seemed like the Reno Coyotes didn't have a single fan in the park.

The game was tied at zero in the second inning. In the first inning, the Coyotes' batters had tried to slug home their base runners, only to be snuffed by the Roadrunner defense. Now, out on the mound, Fumio Kimura, a starting pitcher for the Runners, stomped the rubber and shot a look of disbelief to the ump. He was one ball away from walking his fourth batter in two innings. The

Coyotes were sitting on pitches.

Nick poked his pointer finger into the center of his mitt, telling Fumio where to put a fastball. Fumio shook it off. Nick punched it in again, but Fumio looked away. His choice had already settled in his mind as he kicked into his windup.

It was an inside breaking ball close to the edge, and sure enough the batter let it go by. Without even waiting for the call, the batter tossed his bat behind him and headed to first. Fumio turned so red Nick could see it from home plate.

The Coyotes' next batter was big, with long limbs that flapped up and down like wings as he readied his bat. He was a hard-chopper named Jimenez. Nick watched Jimenez's fingers wring and wrap around the bat and knew that the guy was ready to hit.

Nick also could see from Fumio's death grip on the ball that he was finally ready to bring the heat. But now wasn't the time. He flipped up his fingers, warning Fumio to keep it low, but Fumio put everything he had into a shot over the plate. Jimenez took a small rocking step and put the bat into it. The ball seared a deep arc in the air before disappearing over the left-field wall.

Harris was on his way out to the mound before the ball hit the ground. Nick was there to meet Harris when he arrived.

"It's not working," Harris said to Fumio. He stuck out his hand for the ball. Fumio handed it to him and walked back to the dugout with his head down.

It was Shotaro after that. Nick felt it was a good call. Shotaro's mix of well-aimed speed, off-speed pitches, and deceptive delivery might mess with their bats.

"Just ease it in there during warm-up," Nick told Shotaro when he joined them on the mound. "Then bring the heat."

Nick hurried back into position behind home. From the corner of his eye he watched the batter, a younger player named Erik Mendenhaus, flex into a pretend swing at each warm-up pitch. He was settling into the pitcher's rhythm from a distance, just like

Nick had seen him do since Little League. Local tournaments like this one brought more area players, and Nick knew many of them. Some had tells Nick could use to help the team.

As the game continued, Nick enjoyed watching Mendenhaus swing a whole half-second behind Shotaro's fastball. Mendenhaus then went early against the following changeup. By the time Shotaro caught him swinging under a high fastball, Mendenhaus didn't know if he was coming or going.

Shotaro had been Nick's best friend since the day they met. They often used signs they didn't share with the rest of the team. Nick sent one now, grabbing a small scoop of dirt with his free hand and patting it in a small mound directly behind home plate. Shotaro smirked as he received the message.

Let's bury 'em.

CHAPTER 2

Shotaro had done his part, getting the Roadrunners off the field through the fourth inning with no more runs scored. Now the offense was doing its part. The umpire's narrow strike zone worked both ways, and the Coyotes' pitcher's innings of getting the Roadrunners to chase were over.

Now, as the pitcher tired, most of his strikes ended up in the same place, low and inside. Once the Runners had figured that out, the hitting got easier. The defense managed to clamp down on Sammy Perez with a fly out before Carlos "Trip" Costas punched one through the infield for a single, opening the floodgates. Danny Manuel ripped one down the third baseline that the fielder couldn't get to, and that was followed up with a bloop just over the second baseman by Zack Waddell. That loaded the bases for Nick with one out.

"Knock 'em home, Nico!" came a voice from the stands—Nick's dad, it had to be, in between jobs fixing slot machines on the Strip. No one but his family called him Nico.

The first pitch came in on the hands, and Nick pulled back to keep from getting his wrist crushed by ball one. There was a time Nick might have thought every brush-back was personal, but now he just shrugged it off.

Overcorrect to the outside, Nick thought, *and I'll crush it.*

As the pitch came in, it was just like he'd imagined it, a fat curve hanging on the outside edge of the plate. Nick blasted it just inside the first base line and into right field. The hit had so much spin that it bit into the grass and took a sharp bounce over the foul line, speeding toward the wall's outer edge. A faster runner could have stretched it into a triple, but Nick was content with hustling around to a standing double. All the runners ahead of Nick had much quicker legs, and they motored around the base paths. By the time the right fielder could run down the ball and get it in to the catcher, all three had scored.

"Way to go, Nico! Woo-hoo!" Nick's dad yelled again. "Keep it going, Runners!"

Nick pulled his cap down over his thick black eyebrows. It was a little embarrassing.

After getting the force on Shotaro at first for the second out, the Coyotes' coach called a conference with the pitcher and the catcher, a guy named Derek Kolchak. Derek liked to talk with his hands, with lots of pointing. They were trying to work the pitcher out of the inning and deciding how to pitch to Darius McKay. Darius had the ability to mash one not just over the fence, but through the parking lot if he could get one full contact.

Despite the closed huddle, Nick saw

Derek's hands showing the strike zone and waving beside it. They were going to keep the ball on the outside to see if Darius would swing at bad pitches.

Good strategy, Nick thought. *If you walk Darius, you just put the force in play on me and pitch to the next guy.*

Nick took off his cap and brushed his hair, the team signal for "Pay Attention." Darius stepped back off the plate and watched, pretending to take a practice swing. Nick grabbed his wrist and acted like he was twisting his batting glove on tighter.

Darius nodded. *Hold tight.*

When the first pitch landed, Nick was afraid Darius had been baited because he cranked back with the bat. But he checked his swing, like he'd barely changed his mind in time. He kept it up for two more pitches, riding the count to a fast 3–0.

Nick could see the pitcher was already resigned on a walk. Nick slapped his thigh, and Darius's eyes grew wide. They were going to win the ballgame right here and now.

CHAPTER 3

Shotaro had to wait until after Nick and Darius were done running before they could celebrate together. Darius had done exactly what Nick had hoped. Instead of hanging back and taking the standard 3–0 pitch over the plate like most batters, Darius put everything he had into it. The pitch was so lazy, so fat, that the sound of the aluminum bat on the ball was little more than a *plink* before it was off and gone. The two-run homer put the Runners ahead, where they stayed for the rest of the game. Still, for going against accepted baseball strategy, Harris had sent Nick and Darius on a couple laps around the ballpark.

"One and oh as a starter, baby!" Shotaro said, smacking Nick on his sweaty back. Shotaro's game-face smirk was still in force.

"Five good innings or not, coming in early second inning means a no-start." Nick countered.

"Whatever, man," Shotaro said. "I call it a quality start."

"Congrats on the win," Darius chimed in. "Gotta feel good to get your first one of the season, right?"

"You better believe it," Shotaro said. "Although I had a lot of help."

He gave Nick a fist bump.

"How did you know that little guy would take on a full count?" Shotaro continued. "You are like some sort of baseball psychic!"

Nick smiled. "Dude's a scrawny five-footer in a game with a tight strike zone. Soon as he hunches down too low to swing properly, I know he's holding out for a ball."

"That's what I'm talking about," Shotaro said. "You, me, we're unstoppable. I'm seriously ready to start. We should tell Coach."

Darius wisely broke away toward the dugout to go grab his glove. There was a part of Nick that wished he were right behind him.

"I don't know, Shotaro" Nick answered. "We've got another game coming up in just a few hours. I need to grab some food, change my uniform, and be thinking about that game."

Shotaro's smirk disappeared. "What's to think about? Just go ask Coach to throw me in the rotation. I know he listens to you."

It was true that Coach Harris gave Nick a greater level of influence on game decisions than most coaches would. But Harris wasn't like most coaches, and Nick had proven himself by giving spot-on analysis of batters backed by his almost obsessive stat-tracking of the team. It was a privileged position Nick didn't want to waste on something so uncertain.

Nick started walking back toward the rest of the team, but Shotaro blocked his path.

"It was a good game, Shotaro," Nick said, "but you can't build a case on it. String a bunch of good innings together over a few games to build—"

"A solid ERA," Shotaro jumped in. "I know where you're going with this. Screw the numbers, Nick! That wasn't just a good game; that was a *great* game. The kind of game that a draft scout would notice. He wouldn't care if I improved my average against batters with names beginning with *A* or whatever you track in your little notebook. He'd see I came up in a high-pressure situation with men on base, fanned a bunch of hard-hitting grunts and allowed only four hits in five innings, and he'd hand me his card.

"But that'd be a whole lot more likely to happen if I got a shot at doing it as a starter! You know I've been dreaming about making the rotation since last year. It's what we've been working towards."

Nick rubbed his hand through his thick black hair. Of course that's what they'd hoped for—to be starters. Nick knew better than anyone how much Shotaro had improved, but his gut told him Shotaro wasn't ready yet.

"Look, man. You're just still more likely to have success as a reliever, I think," Nick finally said. "If you want to put on your best performance for a scout, you should do it in a way that plays to your strength. Come in out of the bullpen, dazzle and down some batters with your fastball, and set up the closer for the win."

"So you're not even going to ask Coach?" Shotaro steamed.

Nick had had enough. Shotaro was acting like a little kid. "If you're as good and as ready as you think you are, why don't you just go ask Coach yourself? Why do you even need me?"

"Whatever, man." Shotaro looked away from Nick. "Maybe I don't need you."

CHAPTER 4

The notebook Shotaro had mentioned was a waterproof leather cover Nick had brought to each game since Little League. Inside were stacks of paper that Nick filled up weekly. Those pads, stored in shoeboxes under Nick's bed at home, held the details of every game he'd ever been to or played in. Hasty scribbles recorded during the game were expanded later when Nick could relive each play in his mind. He was filling one in now, jotting down the events of their first-round win to get them out of his head before the second round this afternoon, when something caught his eye.

A camera crew was getting out of gold-colored Channel 6 News van near the field. Nick was surprised to see the stylish blonde reporter climb out of the passenger seat. At a baseball tournament Nick would have expected the old sports-reporter guy, McFadden. But this unfamiliar news team seemed to be rushing to get its equipment out and set up. Maybe they were running behind. This group probably didn't know how to find the ballpark.

Nick watched as the news crew set up its equipment near the field, just a few feet away from him. When everything was settled, the reporter messed with her hair and plastered on a smile for the camera.

"I'm at the Las Vegas Invitational, where hundreds of top high-school baseball prospects are showing their stuff this weekend in a two-day tournament," the reporter said to the camera. "It was on fields like this one where our own Dylan Johnson, and Bryce Harper before him, got their starts, playing in games and catching the eyes of scouts before ultimately, as we saw yesterday, getting picked in the baseball draft."

So that's it, Nick realized. *More about Johnson, not the tournament.*

"This year's draft is over, but there's always next year. Scouts are always looking out for the next superstar talent. Who knows? Someone at this tournament may turn out to be the next Bryce Harper! Andrea Donaldson, Channel 6."

The next Bryce Harper? Nick thought. *Could I ever be that good?*

. . .

As the second game of the tournament began, the words of the news reporter still echoed in Nick's ears.

The next Bryce Harper.

As always, Nick turned to his numbers.

He pictured an imaginary baseball card with Harper's high school stats on the back.

No way I could match for power, Nick said to himself, thinking of Harper's five-hundred-foot home runs. *Nobody can take the ball deep like that. I need to hit more like Joe Mauer.*

An imaginary Joe Mauer card flipped over in his mind, showing off Mauer's more than .500 high school batting average.

Well . . . kind of like Mauer. I'd still need to . . .

"Nick! Get in the on-deck circle!"

Team captain Nellie Carville jammed the batting helmet into Nick's hands and gave him a friendly shove out toward the circle. Nick shook the distraction out of his head. The Runners were ahead of the Huntington Beach Dolphins by six, but that didn't mean he could daydream.

From off to the side of the diamond, Nick got up to speed on the game. Trip was on second with Danny at the plate, and there were no outs yet. The pitcher was throwing off the mark, but it didn't look like he was intentionally walking Danny.

Nick's mind drifted back to his imaginary baseball cards. Dylan Johnson's .997 slugging percentage and thirty home runs loomed large. All those stats seemed unreachable for Nick, except . . .

The sharp *ping*! of Danny's bat brought Nick's eyes back to the game. Danny had ripped one into left field. The outfielder got it, though, and he hurled an impressive rifle shot in to the catcher. Trip was forced to hold up at third while Danny ran around to second.

Nick took his position in the batter's box and waited to see if they would pitch out to him.

Runs batted in, Nick thought. *That's where I can catch those guys.*

Nick was surprised and pleased to see the pitcher whip one in over the plate low for a strike. No easy walks—this guy was going for each batter. It worked perfectly into Nick's plan. With a deep ball to right field, Nick could add two more RBIs to his already fast start this season.

Fifty RBIs this traveling season, Nick realized, *would outpace Harper, Johnson, and Mauer.*

As he watched the next pitch come in high and out of the strike zone, Nick realized he hadn't been studying this pitcher like he should have been.

The next pitch looked like it might be some kind of breaking ball, but it hung straight and Nick's swing met it late. The ball he hoped to put between the first and second baseman instead hit the ground left of the mound and bounced high over the shortstop into left. Nick cursed. The sure-armed left fielder would probably take the ball to third, or maybe to the plate. His potential two-scoring hit wasn't going to pan out.

Nick rounded first and turned for a double before looking to see where the other team was making the play.

"No! Get back! Get back!" yelled Coach Washington, the assistant coach standing at first, as he passed.

Nick was halfway to second before he saw
what had happened. The center fielder had
gotten to the ball before the left fielder and
had thrown the ball to second. Nick slammed
on the brakes and backpedaled to first.
With the first step, Nick could see the first
baseman's eyes tracking the ball in the air. He
wasn't going to be able to make it back in time.
Nick was caught in a rundown.

The second baseman rushed to get rid of
the ball the moment Nick turned back to first.
As soon as the first baseman began to raise
his glove up to receive the throw, Nick headed
back toward second.

Nick had strong legs—catcher's legs—and
he could stop on a dime. But still, they weren't
fast legs. He wasn't nearly close enough to
second to risk a slide. Nick's cleats bit into the
ground as he pushed off again toward first.

The kid playing first was a redhead,
younger than most of the guys, and a long-
armed lefty. His inexperience showed. After
his throw he'd drifted back to the bag instead
of closing the gap between him and his

teammate. The mistake gave Nick just enough room after watching him catch the next throw to leap backwards, just out of reach of a flailing tag.

Still, Nick couldn't get around him to the bag and once again had to change direction. While still watching Nick, the kid made another mistake by faking a throw, trying to get Nick to stop or come back. Instead, Nick turned full-tilt for second as soon as the kid's hand started to pull back off the fake. The first baseman had to completely reset to make the throw, and then he didn't throw accurately.

The ball clipped off Nick's right arm and went wide of the bag. The impact made him stumble slightly and gave the second baseman the chance to make a heads-up play, grabbing and flipping the ball off the grass to the shortstop, who was now at second. Nick pulled up in time, but now there were three players in the mix. With backup behind him, the shortstop came on a dead run for Nick. If he was as fast as he looked, Nick wasn't going to be able to outrun him back to first.

Totally screwed, Nick thought.

The redhead hadn't realized he was out of the play and was still standing just outside the baseline, waiting for a throw. His eyes got wide as he saw Nick dashing toward him even as the shortstop reached out to make the tag. Feeling the heat, Nick laid out for the bag, trying to extend himself beyond the reach of the glove behind him.

Not wanting to be called for interference, the first baseman leaped off the line, throwing his long arms up and out of the way as Nick passed underneath him. On the way up, the tip of the first baseman's glove collided with the shortstop's descending glove. It was enough to knock it off course and prevent the tag by inches. Nick slid safely into first in a spray of dirt.

He rolled over onto his back, keeping his hand firmly on the bag. Safe.

CHAPTER 5

Nick sat on the couch with his parents that evening, wrapped in a half-dozen dishtowels. Between the bumps to his head and shoulders, the games had done a number on his legs and knees. Icepacks, held in place by the towels, were at work on his aching joints and bruises.

Nick and his parents were watching the news, hoping to see the footage of Nick and his dad at the game. The Runners had been on TV before for other games. And by now Nick was so used to it that he didn't really care much. But his parents always liked to watch.

"Ooh, look!" Nick's mom cried. "There it is!"

"*I'm at the Las Vegas Invitational . . .* "

"I hope they show some game clips!" Nick's dad said.

"*So did you see any incredible talent out there today, Andrea?*" one of the news anchors asked.

"*As a matter of fact, check this out.*" Donaldson answered as a clip started up. "*This is from a game our camera crew was at this afternoon.*"

It took Nick a moment to realize what he was seeing.

"Oh my gosh . . ." he said.

"This Nick Cosimo running the bases during the game. Now watch this."

Nick's nimble dodging played out right in front of his eyes. All he could see was poor decision-making and dumb luck, but the anchors were amazed.

"*Unbelievable,*" one said as onscreen Nick dove into first. "*Someone sign this kid right now!*"

Mrs. Cosimo's jazzy ringtone rang out into the living room. She dug in her purse and answered it giddily.

"Hey, Donna! Yeah, I know! I'm saving it on the DVR right now!"

On the table, Nick's own phone started shaking, rattling with a message. Nick saw it was from Shotaro—one of his "I'm not apologizing" texts:

Watching u on TV. Can't B-lieve SS didn't tag ur big butt. U online?

Nick got up from the couch and hobbled to his room to lie down on his bed. His laptop was there, already open. Nick looked at the instant messenger.

Hey, Sho! What's the file you're sending me?

The progress bar was almost full.

News story off Ch. 6 website. U should put it on ur wall. U need to start selling ur self to scouts, d00d.

Adding the clip to the recruitment tape his dad had started wouldn't be a bad idea either.

Nick opened up his master file of baseball stats, updated daily through a web app. He scrolled down to Joe Mauer's name and started cutting and pasting stats into a spreadsheet. Beneath it he started a row for his own numbers.

U c how ez it is to get noticed? Shotaro wrote. *TV should already b talkin about us, tho, not discovering us. We gotta do this.*

Nick added one more thing to his desktop—a countdown widget starting at 312 days. He labeled it "Days Until Eligibility." He looked at his RBI stat, already sitting at eleven early in the season. Tournaments were always unpredictable, of course, but at this pace he might hit not just fifty, but sixty.

We gotta do this, he typed back. *Game on.*

. . .

"Does it look like there are a lot more suits out there watching today than there were yesterday?" Danny asked. The confident center fielder looked more nervous than usual.

The Roadrunners were gathered for one last huddle before the semifinal game began, but the topic had gotten off track.

"Seems like it to me," Gus said. "Ask Nick. He's the numbers guy."

"I don't keep track of that," Nick said, although it was obvious that attendance seemed to be up by a couple hundred people. It was a crowd they usually expected to see at the championship game which wouldn't be until much later this evening.

"Enough, guys," Harris said. "You need to keep your mind on the game, and not on who might be out there scouting you."

"Scouts?" Shotaro piped up. "Which scouts? From where? College or pro?"

"I saw this one bald guy with notebook talking on his cell phone in the stands. He said something about looking for 'real talent,'" Sammy said excitedly.

All the Roadrunners knew Coach Harris had at least one contact with just about every major league team. If someone other than the usual UCLA recruiter was hanging about, Harris would know.

"It's all probably just more fans watching," Harris said.

"Yeah, all Nick's fans," Darius said, jabbing Nick with his elbow. "That clip had twenty thousand hits on it already on YouTube this morning."

"Who put it on YouTube?" said Nick.

"Quiet!" Harris yelled. "We're going out to play in just a few minutes. Get focused."

Everyone quieted down.

"Now, these guys have been putting up some big-time defense this tournament. We have to take advantage of opportunities and clamp down on mistakes. If it's a close game, I want to be ahead. Field team's in, but don't get bent out of shape if I swap in some bats. Questions?"

Danny's hand shot up.

"What is it, D?"

"It's the scout from the Yankees, right?"

"Just get your butt on the field, Danny."

As the team broke the huddle, Shotaro grabbed Nick's arm.

"I wonder if that guy Sammy saw is from the Yankees. I bet there are lots of scouts out there today," he said. "You saw how Coach froze up when we called him on it."

Nick nodded. "You might be right."

"You need to get me in the game," Shotaro said. "I mean, if Dom's pitching is off, try to get me in. I got the stuff today. I know it." Dominic Schmidt was the Runners' solid, all-purpose pitcher.

"Maybe you should tell Coach," Nick offered.

"I'm going to," Shotaro said. "But he really listens to you."

"All right," Nick agreed. "But only if Dom's stuff doesn't hold up. He could pitch a no-hitter today for all we know."

"Yeah, yeah," Shotaro said. "But if he doesn't . . ."

Shotaro pointed to the number on his jersey and then stuck out his thumb and pinky finger to make the "call" sign near his ear.

"I promise," Nick said. "I'll push for you as soon as it gets bad."

"How bad?" Shotaro pressed.

"You know. Bad."

CHAPTER 6

"Okay. This is bad." Nellie rubbed his forehead in frustration.

"At least the inning's over," Nick said.

The team had just come off of a three-error inning that let the Phoenix Sand Demons get a pair of runs. It had started with Danny muffing a routine fly ball while trying to turn it into a showy catch. And it got worse from there. The Roadrunners tried too hard to compensate for the screw-up by later trying to nail down a double play on a hit to shortstop. Trip stomped the bag for the force but overthrew Gus at first, letting the runner take second. Following a walk, Sammy charged up on a fast bouncing grounder only to let it get behind him and roll to the wall for a triple.

"Man, I *hope* there aren't any scouts out there," Sammy mumbled, mostly to himself.

"We've just got to get it out of our minds," Nick said. But even as he put on his helmet and moved to the circle, he scanned the crowd. There was a guy in the front row with olive khakis and so much sunscreen on his bald head it glimmered in the light. He must have been the guy Sammy had seen before the game. Nick had spotted him earlier. He'd also caught Harris and Wash looking at him. The guy took pictures and talked into a voice recorder with each batter. And any time anyone made a big play, the man had scribbled like mad in a notebook. He was making notes now, probably because Danny had just gone down swinging on three straight pitches.

Nick straightened his batting helmet and stepped up to the plate. He was determined to turn things around against a pitcher who seemed to be on top of his game. The Sand Demon catcher chuckled as Nick came up to bat. The catcher was someone Nick knew from school, Chris Henderson. Henderson had already been kicked off of two teams for fighting. He was generally a grade-A jerk. His family moved to Arizona so he could play with the Sand Demons. If Henderson didn't consistently bat .450 and hit twenty-plus homers a year, he probably wouldn't be able to find a team that would take him.

"Hey, Cosimo," Henderson said as Nick got in his stance. "I heard you were playing for the other team."

Nick said nothing, but let the first pitch pass by for a ball on the inside. Henderson tossed back the ball.

"But then again, I guess you're always playing for the other team, right?"

For a moment, Nick wondered if the scout knew. Nick was out, certainly, but it wasn't something you'd know by watching him play baseball. He'd always figured that a scout would only find out that he was gay if he was actively looking at Nick, which at least meant he'd already be interested.

"Wow, I never heard that one before," Nick said without looking at Chris. The next pitch was a fastball, and Nick fouled it up and over the backstop.

"Cut that chatter, you two," the umpire yelled. "Or I'll eject you both."

Chris kept his tongue in check, and Nick checked his swing as the next pitch seemed to pass just outside. The umpire called it a strike. A strange thought popped into Nick's head.

What if the scout was a guy like Henderson?

The brief distraction was enough to make Nick chop roughly at the next pitch and miss it. Nick banged the bat on the ground in disgust while Chris stood up and threw the ball around the horn with a triumphant gleam in his eye.

CHAPTER 7

The game was an equal-opportunity disaster, and Shotaro got the chance to replace Dom in the third inning. He'd already fanned one batter. Maybe this was the turnaround moment.

All right, thought Nick. *Let's see if we can't get weak contact on an off-speed pitch.* He flashed the signal to Shotaro, but Shotaro shrugged it off and went into his motion. It was another fastball, as fast as it'd ever gone. The batter came around way too slow. Nick repeated the signal, but again Shotaro gave a slight shake of the head and wound up. This time the fastball had a low breaking movement, and the batter swung above it.

Nick made an exaggerated call for a curve. But yet another fastball tinked off the edge of the bat and into his mitt for strike three.

"Time!" Nick called to the ump and ran out to the mound.

"What are you doing?" Shotaro said. "I'm just getting into rhythm."

"And soon they'll start picking up on it. You can't go full speed full time."

Shotaro sniffed. "How about you just go back and let me do my job? I'll own these guys."

Some jerks like Chris teased Shotaro, saying he was Nick's boyfriend. But that wasn't true. At first Nick and Shotaro had been good friends who'd met on a youth league team. They had since thrown thousands of practice pitches in each other's backyards. When Nick had come out in ninth grade, it had been as hard for him to get up the courage to tell Shotaro as it had been to tell his family. Shotaro hadn't even blinked.

"You want a hug or a medal or something? Hurry up and go get your glove."

That's when Nick knew they were best friends. There was no question that Nick could tell Shotaro anything. The problem was that if those things were about Shotaro, then Shotaro usually didn't listen.

Out of the corner of his eye, Nick saw Harris take a step out of the dugout. If Harris figured out Shotaro was trying to impress scouts, Shotaro would be sitting for sure.

"Fine," Nick said, and went back toward home. Harris sat back down as well.

At least Shotaro was open to suggestion on locations. As Nick predicted, the Sand Demons started getting down the timing after one or two innings. Only Shotaro's skillful placement kept them guessing and hitting into playable balls.

As the top of the order for the Sand Demons came around, Nick called for a sinking fastball. A moment later, he watched in horror as Shotaro hung the pitch right over the center of the plate. The batter crushed it for a liner single.

Henderson was the next batter up. He grinned at Nick.

"Your boyfriend's arm is starting to fall off," he said. "I'm taking the first pitch downtown."

"Shut up, punk!" Nick growled.

"Last warning, both of you," the ump declared.

Nick knew Chris was right. Shotaro's speed and control were fading fast. He crossed his fingers and called for Shotaro to throw a curve on the outside. Henderson would either chase or let it go for a ball. Either way, he wouldn't be hitting the first ball like he'd promised.

Having shifted to the outside edge of the plate, Nick had to lunge unexpectedly to the inside in hopes of keeping Shotaro's pitch from getting behind him. It wasn't even close to what Nick had called for.

He didn't have to worry about a passed ball though. Good to his word, Henderson walloped it. It wasn't a home run, but it was good enough for an easy double.

Shotaro would have to listen to reason now. Nick repeated the call for an outside curve on the next batter. He watched Shotaro's face redden in anger, but also saw him nod. Perhaps he realized a scout wouldn't be impressed with him at this point.

Probably not with me either, Nick thought. *But their guy is slowing down a little, too. If he leads with a sinker I can . . .*

The pitch was all muscle and poorly forced, rising too high. Nick broke from his thoughts and jumped up for the unexpected fastball, but he was an instant behind. The pitch flew behind him into the backstop. Nick heard it spring away somewhere and ripped off his mask to look for it. By the time he'd spotted the ball and picked it up, another run had scored. Shotaro had run in to cover home and was glaring at him.

"What are you doing, man?" Shotaro barked. "That was a catchable ball! Where's your head?"

Behind Shotaro, Harris was again coming out of the dugout. This time, Nick knew, he wouldn't be turning around.

CHAPTER 8

Shotaro sat on the very end of the bench, arms crossed tight and cap pulled down over his eyes as Nick went out to bat. The conversation of who was at fault for the passed ball would have to wait. Coach Harris's prediction of a low-scoring defensive battle had flown right out the window. With a five-run lead, the Sand Demons had lost some power, fielding one-hoppers they might have caught with a full effort if the game had been tighter.

The tiring Sand Demons' starter was still pitching, letting the thin trickle of runners grow to a steady stream as the Roadrunners clawed their way back into the game. Down only three with runners at the corners and one out in the bottom of the third, Nick had a chance to put the team within striking distance.

Danny was taking an extended lead off of first. The pitcher didn't seem to notice. He was focused on whatever pitch Henderson was signaling and taking a long time to get to it. The opportunity was there. Wash saw it, too, and called for the hit and run. Nick dropped into his stance and readied himself to punch it through, maybe even get the runner home from third.

The pitcher wound up and Danny took off. The delivery was fast, as fast as Nick had seen it all game, and it came streaking right at his head. Nick fell backward out of the way. Henderson was already on his feet to receive the ball, and he hurled it to second. It was a perfect throw. The baseman tagged Danny on the slide with ease.

Did Henderson tell the pitcher to headhunt?
Was it to get at me or the runner?

Nick would probably never know. He refused to back off the plate, though, and ripped the next pitch up the left side. It should have been good for a hit, but the third baseman made an incredible play in catching the ball for the last out of the inning. With his last at bat come and gone, Nick was now a miserable 0 for 2.

Travis Melko, the current reliever, was still in the on-deck circle as Nick passed.

"Tough break, bro," he said. "Good hit."

"Whatever," Nick grumbled.

"Top of the order coming up," Travis said. "How should we play 'em?"

"Do whatever," Nick said. "Just don't go too fast between pitches. Cool them down."

"All right," Travis said. "Maybe you should cool down some yourself, Nick. You seem a little pissed."

Nick tried to push his irritation with himself deeper to the background. He hated losing, especially to a jerk like Henderson, who was next up to bat for the Sand Demons.

Travis looked to Nick for the call. Henderson wasn't going for anything outside the strike zone, and he was getting pieces of everything inside it. Nick signaled for a high curve at the inside corner. But the pitch drifted in too far, and Henderson let it pass by for ball three. Rather than throw it back, Nick held onto it. Henderson wasn't the only one who could play mind games. Nick signaled for the outfielders to come in. Remembering Henderson's last hit, the three of them took only a few uncertain steps forward. Nick then dramatically waved at them to come in further, even though Wash was signaling them to stay put.

"You're playing with fire now," Henderson mumbled softly.

"Play ball," the ump said.

Nick threw the ball back to Travis and then sent the signal. Travis blinked but nodded. He set himself and began his motion. Henderson flexed his grip and readied to swing. The pitch came sailing in off the outside edge of the plate. Expecting it to curve in toward him like the previous pitches, and eager to smash one over the dangerously shallow outfielders, Henderson swung. The pitch failed to turn in, staying outside of the strike zone, and Henderson missed it. He'd been tricked into chasing a bad pitch.

"Too easy. I thought you were a pro, Henderson," Nick said.

Henderson dropped the bat and grabbed for Nick's jersey, pulling him close. Without thinking, Nick took a swing at Henderson's face. But Henderson dodged, and Nick just grazed his ear.

"That's it!" the ump shouted, stepping between them. "Take a walk. I'm tossing both of you."

Nick started walking. He was going to catch all sorts of trouble for this, but he smiled anyway. In just this moment, it was totally worth it.

. . .

At home, Nick had been grounded for getting ejected. The only area where he got his parents to budge was in getting permission to go off to the batting cage. Nick had "forgotten" to mention that the batting cage was in Trip's half-acre backyard, behind the pool and beach volleyball court. He promised himself that he would get in a few swings before he left. First he'd have to wait for the partygoers to clear out.

"Man, I still can't believe you got thrown out," Trip said, tossing Nick an energy drink. "I don't think that's ever happened before."

"It hasn't," Nick replied. "But Henderson was giving me the 'homo' crap again, so I pushed back."

"At least he got ejected too," Trip said with a nod. "But people give you that crap all the time, even when they don't know you're gay. What was the difference now?"

"There was this scout . . ." Nick trailed off, unsure of his answer.

"There's always a scout. Comes with the turf."

"It just hit me different today, Trip," Nick mused. "I got to wondering whether being gay goes on a scouting report. You know, if the scout knew."

"Does it matter?" Trip said. "It's the twenty-first century. People kinda get that there are gay people around."

"We're not just talking people," Nick said. "We're talking pro athletes."

A well-tanned girl with long, dark hair swayed over next to them, bobbing in time to the music pulsing from the outdoor speakers. She was wearing a trio of sparkling necklaces over a sleeveless black top.

"Heyyyy, Trip . . ." she said. "How about you get some club music going? I wanna dance! This hip-hop thing's getting old."

"Better take it up with the DJ, Ashley. I'm not picking the songs."

"I will," Ashley smiled. "But promise to come dance with me, Trip?"

"Sure thing," Trip said as the girl breezed away on four-inch heels.

Nick continued, "You think the Twins

would still have taken Joe Mauer if he'd been gay?"

"Sure. Big hometown hero."

"Yeah, but would he still have been as big of a hometown hero if he'd been openly gay in high school?"

"Guess I don't know, man." He glanced toward the house. "I better go meet Ashley, though."

Nick gave Trip a fist bump. "Alright, man. Thanks."

"Hey, where's Sho tonight?" Trip asked.

"Who knows? He's mad at me for the game or something."

Trip smiled. "That kid is such a stubborn punk sometimes."

Nick just shrugged.

CHAPTER 9

Nick didn't know if he and Shotaro had ever been on a bus without sitting together, whether it was a school bus in junior high or a decked-out charter bus like this one. That wasn't a stat in his notebook. But since Shotaro was still mad and Nick wasn't feeling forgiving, he sat in back. Shotaro was in front by himself with a pair of headphones over his ears. Like most of the players who chose to ride the "Big Mama" to their next tournament in Flagstaff, Arizona, Shotaro was watching ESPN. Most of the seat-back TVs were tuned into the station through the bus's satellite dish.

Sammy, on the other hand, had surrounded himself with textbooks. Nick couldn't remember the last time he'd seen Sammy study. It was shaping up to be a weird day.

"Taking summer school or something?" Nick asked. Sammy bent the corner of the page he was on and closed the book.

"Nah," Sammy answered. "I'm thinking about maybe taking the GED, getting it out of the way, you know?"

"Taking the GED doesn't matter in the NCAA," Nick said. "You still have to send your grades and stuff, I think."

"I don't think college is for me," Sammy said. "School always seems to be in the way, and I'm thinking big time."

From the seat behind Nick, Trip leaned up over the backrest. Nick often marveled at how much Trip looked like his dad, the famous singer. But it was only when Trip wasn't in uniform.

"Really, Sammy? I could do with less press hanging around my family," Trip said. "But sometimes I think it would be nice to be done with school and move on to something else."

"Yeah," Sammy said. "Like more baseball! You've got some offers coming in, yeah?"

Based on Nick's estimation, Trip had more of a chance at going pro than anyone on the team but Sammy. But Trip never seemed excited by the idea.

"Some," Trip said. "But it might be nice to have something else in my life besides baseball."

"And what about you, Nick Pickle?" Sammy teased. "You've been tearing it up this season . . ."

Nick shot him an annoyed look, in part for using the new YouTube-inspired nickname.

". . . you know, for the most part, so far. Last game aside," Sammy added.

From across the aisle, Gus laughed. "Nick's already got all he needs. He just needs college recruiters to see the video!"

Nick rolled his eyes. The rundown clip

was picking up steam on the Internet, to the point of getting spoofed. One creative duo had digitally replaced Nick with a frantic, flapping chicken.

"You've also been going nuts with the notes," Trip continued. "You got an angle on a career move or what?"

Nick thumbed at the leather cover to his notes, but he didn't need to look at them. He knew exactly where he stood. Sure, he was still on pace for fifty RBIs this traveling season, but that might not be enough anymore. His hits and on-base percentages might not be enough. He pictured the countdown on his computer, ticking down the days to draft eligibility.

"I dunno," Nick said. "Still looking for that magic formula, I guess."

. . .

It was purely by accident that Nick spotted him again. During fielding practice, Wash popped a foul straight up for Nick to catch.

He ripped off his catcher's mask, turned, and tracked the ball. After catching it, he looked down and into the stands behind home plate.

There he was, the same bald guy who had been showing up to their other games. Wash noticed Nick looking out and followed his gaze. Once Wash spotted the man, though, he quickly turned back to hitting more flies. Nick rolled the ball he'd caught over near Wash's feet.

"So what do you think?" Nick asked Wash. "Are we being stalked or are we being scouted?"

Wash gave him a quick, nervous glance and hit a fly to the outfield.

"I wouldn't worry about it," Wash said.

"But you know him," Nick said.

"Not personally," Wash answered. "But yeah, I know who he is."

"Is he a scout?" Nick asked.

Wash paused between hits, weighing his answer.

"Yeah, he's a scout. A big numbers guy," Wash told him. "You two might get along. But if I was you I'd worry less about him and more about these balls coming in."

. . .

As soon as the fielding practice was over, Nick hurried over to where most of the pitchers were tossing balls back and forth.

"Shotaro," Nick called. "Hey! Listen!"

Shotaro barely paid him any attention.

"What is it? You finally manage to get your head out of your butt?"

"That guy Sammy saw the other day, the scout, he's back!"

Shotaro gave a dismissive flip of the ball to his partner.

"I'm so happy for you," he said.

"This could work out for you too," Nick said. "There's a chance you could get in today."

"You know as well as I do it doesn't matter if it was five days ago," Shotaro shot back. "Coach doesn't send in pitchers two games in a row."

"He won't send *starters* out two games in a row," Nick said quickly, "but sometimes he—"

He had said the words so quickly he hadn't thought it through. Shotaro's pitching hand gripped the ball so tightly his knuckles turned white.

"Right," Shotaro jumped in. "And I'm *not* a starter, am I?"

Nick wanted to smack himself in the head.

"I didn't mean that," Nick said. "I'm just saying we've got a chance to—"

"There's no *we* today, Nick," Shotaro said, turning back. "So how about you go do your thing and I'll do mine. I don't need your help."

It hurt that Shotaro was shutting him out this way. But Shotaro was probably right. He stood little chance of pitching this game. Maybe, for now, Nick should think about himself.

CHAPTER 10

Nick had decided that for now his plan to win over the scouts was going to be little different than how he'd won over his teammates. Over the years most of them had come to grips with his being gay pretty well. Reactions were mostly variations on a theme, with even those who had always believed themselves open-minded still having to reboot their brains for a moment. Once they'd re-categorized Nick and everything they'd ever done together with him, they'd usually mumble something like, "That's cool . . ." Over time, many came to believe it.

Those friends or teammates who might have been more bothered by it found it hard to argue with results. Nick tended to be near the top in batting average every season.

This was one of those games, and it sucked that he couldn't share it with his best friend. Nick had just finished gunning down another runner trying to steal second. When he looked back over at the bench at Shotaro, as if to say *Hey, did you see that*, it was clear that Shotaro hadn't.

It helped that the batter hadn't swung. He seemed to be waiting for "a good one."

If Shotaro had been in the game, Nick would have given a quick pound on the ground with his fist, another secret sign that meant "dive bomber." As it was, he felt pitcher Carson Jamison had control enough to get the job done. Nick made a call for a sinker.

Carson nodded and let the ball fly. It looked like a fat fastball coming in slightly high, but by the time the batter started coming around with his swing it dove into the dirt at the front of home plate. The batter missed by a mile for strike three.

"Nice pitching," Nick called to Carson as they left the infield.

"Yeah, I know," Carson said with a grin.

"How's your arm holding up?"

The grin dropped.

"Just fine," Carson said. "Why do you ask?"

"I'm just checking," Nick said quickly. "We're already up by four, and we're hitting well. There's no reason to push it if your pitch count's getting up there."

"Don't worry about me," Carson said. "I can chuck it all day long."

But Nick didn't give up. The other team, the Marshals, were from Fort Worth and had come to this tournament in Flagstaff fresh off a trip to Baton Rouge. They were playing like they were jetlagged—easy pickings from the pitcher's mound. It could do a lot for Shotaro's confidence if he could just get in the game.

Nick plopped down on the bench next to Coach Harris.

"I think we should start thinking relief," Nick said.

"Take an antacid," Harris said flatly.

"I think Shotaro could really work these guys," Nick said.

"My great aunt could work these guys right now, and she's over eighty and dead."

"But I was thinking—"

"Carson stays in until they start tagging him," Harris said. "We're done now. Sit down."

Nick sat down on the bench next to Shotaro anyway.

"I tried," Nick said.

Shotaro didn't even look at him.

CHAPTER *11*

The Marshals' pitcher wasn't doing his team any favors. After Trip doubled off a weak curve to start the inning, the guy had walked two to load the bases.

Nick considered him as he stepped up to the plate. The guy was tall—really tall— probably six and a half feet. He had a strange, whiplike sidearm throw that on better days probably gave him a good combination of speed and motion. Today wasn't one of those days, though. Nick watched the first pitch fly too far from left to right and end up on the outside of the plate.

"Ball," came the call.

Nick lifted his bat back up and gave it a wiggle, keeping his arms loose. A hit right now, with the bases loaded, could pad Nick's stats. The pitcher took his motion slower, dropping his arm into an almost submarine throw that rose too high and out of the strike zone.

"Ball," the ump again intoned.

Nick noticed that Wash was keeping the runners near the bags. Wash wanted the pitcher to get some strikes across before Nick swung and walk in a run if he couldn't.

With an overhand throw, the long-armed hurler threw to first. With Zack hugging the bag it was a pointless move, but the pitcher repeated it a few times without even trying to mask it. A few observers in the crowd booed.

A light went on in Nick's head. The pitcher wasn't trying to catch the runner off the bag. He was stretching and fine-tuning his arm before throwing his next pitch. When the pitcher finally cranked his arm back in what looked to be a more overhand delivery, Nick knew he was right.

It came in middle high, and Nick belted a low-arcing ball to the right-side gap. The right fielder rushed in with a chance to make a play on it, dove, and just missed getting his glove under it. The center fielder was in position to back up his teammate, but by the time he got the ball in to second, two runs had scored and Zack had made it around to third.

Nick had held up at first, not risking getting beat by the throw to second. He then took a moment to check out the scout, who was marking up a yellow legal pad. Seemed like a good sign.

"Be a shame if we mercy rule these guys," Nick whispered to Wash, out of earshot of the baseman. "We're getting some great numbers off them."

Wash didn't answer. His eyes locked on Nick, and then he looked toward the field ump.

"Time," he said. "Substitution."

Nick's eyebrows nearly relocated to the top of his head.

"What?" he said, as Wash turned back to him.

"I'm bringing in Dustin to pinch run."

"But then I'm out," Nick protested. He couldn't believe it. Dustin Conover was a fast runner, but not one of the team's strongest players.

"Yeah, you're out," Wash agreed. "Now go sit down."

• • •

The victory party poolside at the hotel was getting festive. Dustin's dad was a high roller too. And after hearing that Dustin got the winning RBI, his dad was more than happy to let Dustin drop a grand on poolside entertainment in the form of a hastily catered buffet and a brand-new karaoke machine. Nellie had just finished a ridiculous Justin Timberlake cover. Trip was now doing a spot-on impression of one of his father's songs.

Nick, on the other hand, was still in his street clothes, pecking away on his laptop by himself in a quiet corner. A shadow fell across his screen. Nick looked up to see his coach standing over him, arms crossed.

"There something going on that I need to know about?" Harris said. Harris often asked questions when he already knew the answer.

"Between me and Shotaro, you mean?" Nick and Shotaro had yet to patch things up, and it was bugging Nick.

"I mean between your left ear and your right ear," Harris answered. "You seemed to have problems keeping your head in the game today."

"Hard to keep my head in the game when the rest of me is out of the game, Coach. Almost cost us. Dustin had no idea how to call that game."

What had seemed like a gimmie win had nearly gotten away from the Runners as the Marshals caught on to the unimaginative fastball, fastball, changeup pattern Dustin and Carson had going. Dustin's "game-winner" wouldn't have even been necessary if he hadn't been calling up meatballs for the other team to hit.

"In the end, he got the job done. And he listened, which is more than you've been doing. I let you get away with making some calls in the field because you've got a gift for seeing the big picture. And, I trust you. But it seems like your focus has been getting a little smaller. Trying for extra bases, swinging when you should be taking, stuff like that. I know you're not padding your stats to impress me, so who are you doing it for? That scout?"

"So you do know he's there? The bald guy?" Nick said, interested now.

"Yeah, I know," Harris admitted, lowering his voice.

"Well, he seems a step above the usual. Would it hurt me to have a good scouting report with someone like that?"

"Look, I think you need to go back to worrying about your team and forget about the Dodgers."

Nick's eyebrows shot up. "The Dodgers?"

Harris heaved a sigh.

"Yeah," Harris said. "He currently works for the Dodgers. Of course, things change. I said forget about it. Let's talk about something else, like the game tomorrow."

Out of the corner of his eye, Nick saw Shotaro land a half-hearted cannonball in the deep end of the pool. Shotaro often was emotional or angry, but wasn't usually a sulker. Not starting must be more important than Nick even realized. Maybe he could give it one more try. . . .

"I think Shotaro should start the next game," Nick said.

"And why's that?" Harris asked.

"We're playing the Sacramento Seagulls tomorrow afternoon. Six of the nine likely starters on that team are left-handed. Shotaro's ERA drops down nearly two full points against lefties, and he's given up fewer runs against lefties per nine innings than anyone else on the team."

Harris gave him a blank look.

"Plus, they have a lot of pull hitters with moderate power in a park with a deep right-field wall. We can get them to fly out."

Harris's look was unchanged.

"I thought you said you trusted me," Nick said. Harris thought about it.

"You do well in math, Nick?"

"Yes sir. Straight As," Nick said. "C in biology, though."

Harris blew a gust of air out his nose.

"All right, you got it," he said. "We'll see how it goes."

Nick pumped his fist as Harris turned his attention to the off-key warbling from his players.

CHAPTER *12*

Despite his years of experience, Nick had just made a rookie mistake and he was now paying for it. He'd left his hamburger alone at the booth while he went to the bathroom. Now it sat buried under a massive pile of pickle slices.

"Cute, guys," Nick said.

"It was Sho's idea," Danny laughed.

Shotaro had been in a much better mood since Nick had told him about his upcoming start. He was back to his old self. He was goofing around with a few players now at an early team lunch before their game against the Sacramento Seagulls.

Nick turned to Shotaro. "You know, we should probably figure out how we're going to play these guys coming up," Nick said.

"You call 'em, I'll throw 'em," Shotaro said with a shrug. "Easy, breezy."

"Will you actually?" Nick pressed.

"Yeah! Yeah, dude, for sure," Shotaro promised. "I left that whole 'scout in the crowd' thing back in Nevada. I just want to get the win."

Nick decided not to tell Shotaro that the scout they'd been seeing was from the Dodgers and would probably be there again today. Nick didn't want to risk it messing with his head. Nick's standing with Harris was linked to Shotaro now. Nick didn't want Shotaro doing anything stupid that would get him, or maybe both of them, pulled.

"I think the secret is keeping them from getting any solid contact," Nick said. "Don't worry so much about strikeouts, and let the defense deal with whatever gets hit."

"Uh, oh," Shotaro said. "Here comes trouble."

Nick turned in the restaurant booth and saw Kurt storming over toward them. It had been Kurt's turn in the rotation until Shotaro got bumped up for the next game. Coach had probably just given him the bad news.

"I know this is your fault," Kurt said, towering over Nick.

"It's nothing against you," Nick said. "I really thought Shotaro might be the better choice going into the game."

"I think that's Coach's decision to make," Kurt replied.

Shotaro stood up from the booth, matching Kurt's height inch for inch.

"I think the coach *did* make a decision," Shotaro said.

"Settle down, guys," Wash said, appearing suddenly and stepping between them.

"Take nothing for granted in baseball," Wash said. "No promises, no guarantees."

The guys backed off, but Kurt still glared at Nick.

"Just because you're not starting doesn't mean you aren't pitching," Wash continued. "So you'd better be ready to go today, understand?"

"Understood," Kurt said. He didn't give them another look as he strode out of the restaurant.

"You've got to shut these things down early," Wash warned. "If people start thinking you're only in it for yourself, it can split up a team pretty quick."

Nick nodded, taking a nervous sip from his straw.

"Even faster if it's true," Wash said.

. . .

Wash's words were finally being drowned out by the steady rhythm of pitches smacking into Nick's mitt. The Runners went three up and three down in the first inning against the Seagulls.

"Strike!" the ump yelled. The Seagulls' first batter was waiting for his pitch. He was going to have to keep waiting. Nick called for the same pitch, and Shotaro painted the inside corner with even greater speed than the first one for strike two.

The batter stepped out of the batter's box, spat on the ground angrily, and again crouched in at the plate.

Too eager, Nick thought, sending the signal. Shotaro nodded and double-timed his wind-up and release. The batter split the air with his bat even before the slower changeup reached the plate.

It had been going well so far. Nick's take on the deeper wall seemed to be on the money. The first and third batters had gotten a solid bat on the ball, but both times Sammy had caught them well within the right field warning track instead of watching the ball sail over his head for a home run.

Still, we're gonna want to keep those heavy hits down.

Nick had Shotaro wing one in high, and

the newest batter fouled it back. Shotaro had worked the strike zone brilliantly. Nick called for one outside, trying to get the batter to chase, but his eye was too good.

Time to bring the heat, Nick thought. Shotaro put his fastball in faster and lower, but still just outside the plate. This time, the batter came around and connected. The ball slammed into the ground right in front of the plate and launched into the air toward third. Nellie was underneath to bring in the ball as soon as it came down again, but it was too late to throw it to first.

The hit had kicked up dirt onto the plate, so the umpire took a moment to brush it off. Nick used the pause to take a quick look around the stands. He hadn't seen the scout yet, but he felt sure he was there somewhere.

A giant was at the plate next—six and a half feet easy. The Roadrunners had played this team last year, but this kid was new. His name was Brian Krzynski, a sophomore, and he looked like he could hit a ball a long way. Nick called an outfield shift to move back and then sent a sign for Shotaro to keep the ball up high. Shotaro fired off a fastball so high that Nick had to push up on his heels.

But even that pitch wasn't high enough, coming in level with Krzynski's shoulders, and he swung on it. The ball took off like a missile. It had a low angle but more than enough muscle behind it. In about two seconds it would clear the left-field wall.

CHAPTER *13*

The base runner assumed he'd hit a home run and was on his way to second. He had the best view in the park to see Darius use his unbelievable speed to meet the ball at the wall and yank it out of the air with a perfect leap. The runner scrambled to turn around and run back to first.

Nick breathed a sigh of relief. He was amazed that a hit at that low level could travel that far. He called the outfield in closer for the next batter, a bony outfielder. In the top of the first, he'd run in to catch a hit that usually would have dropped for a single.

He was patient, too. He sat on the first three pitches for two strikes and a ball before finally taking a swing at a changeup. It popped up into the sky and flew overhead into left.

Although he was already playing in, Darius took one step forward off the weak sound of the bat before changing his mind and beginning to retreat. A moment later he was running backward to get into position.

Nick could hardly believe it. The ball should not have been carrying that far. Darius was in position to make the third out, but only after running to the warning track again.

As the Roadrunners left the field, Nick was distracted. How'd the ball go so far? Had they moved the fence in from last year? He hoped one of his teammates might crush one deep to judge the distance it traveled.

If the first two innings were any indicator, however, that didn't seem likely.

"Man, he's throwing nasty stuff," Danny said. He'd battled to a full count before getting sat down on a called third strike on the inside to start off the top of the second.

"Yeah, but he's also thrown eleven balls already," Nick said, walking on deck. "All movement, no control."

"If no one can hit him, how much control does he need?" Danny wondered.

The Seagulls' pitcher proved it again by getting Zack on a diving fastball. As Nick stepped into the box, he could see the pitcher was confident.

It was a good bet the first pitch thrown would be a strike, so Nick committed to swing. As the ball came in, Nick got a bead on it and swung, only to have it cut down and away. Nick was amazed by how the ball seemed to turn in the air. It had started inside the strike zone but moved outside. It was the most movement he'd ever seen on a pitch.

And it gave Nick an idea.

The next pitch also seemed to be coming right down the pipe. Nick didn't flinch. Like before, the ball veered away and dropped out of the strike zone for a ball. Nick took a step back and took a cut with his bat, keeping his arms loose. He stepped back in and waited. The next pitch started more inside, but was way too low. When it crossed the plate, it was barely higher than Nick's ankles.

The 2–1 pitch was the one he was waiting for, thrown inside at his elbows. Nick swung, having faith that the ball wasn't going to stay inside and bean his arm.

It didn't. Like the others, the pitch cut away, this time swerving into the strike zone where Nick was swinging. He blasted the ball straight back at the pitcher. The pitcher tried to duck. The ball blazed by his shoulder as he hunched and brought up his arms to protect his head. It passed over second base and dropped into the outfield.

The center fielder must have gotten to the ball quick enough to think he had a play. As Nick crossed the bag, the first baseman jumped into the air. The throw had come in high for him to reach, and it flew past him. Nick turned the corner and dashed to second.

From second base, looking back, he took in the plate, the stands, and the sky. The tall flagpole standing at the entrance to the parking lot was visible, and the American flag flapped wildly. It took Nick a moment before the significance of it hit him.

There's a tail wind, Nick realized.

The Flagstaff ballpark was basically a bowl, surrounded on all sides. It sat in the middle of a stretch of flat, sandy earth. There were no trees and not a cloud in the sky. There was nothing to show that the breeze had picked up and was now blowing over the top of the ballpark. Inside the park you couldn't feel a thing, but a high-hit ball would get extra distance now.

Now up to bat, Shotaro chased a ball and dribbled it up the first baseline for the second out. Darius grounded out next. Nick gave Shotaro the news about the wind as soon as he got back to the dugout.

"We might be screwed," Nick told him. "The wind's come up since the game started."

CHAPTER *14*

*I*t didn't take long for Nick's fears to be realized. The Seagulls' first batter, a lefty, managed to get around on a 2–2 inside pitch and put it up just fair over first. Nick could almost see the ball being pushed outward as soon as it had cleared the height of the park's outer walls. It didn't clear the fence for a homer, but it still banged off the barrier before Sammy could get it back into the infield to hold the runner at second.

Shotaro's first pitch to the next batter came in chin-high for a ball.

I shouldn't have said anything, Nick thought. *I should have just changed the pitch calls. Now Shotaro's nervous about getting rocked.*

The second pitch was also too high. The Roadrunners needed to get these bottom-order players out. The worst thing that could happen would be for the top of the order to come up with runners on and no outs.

Nick hoped that the batter might sit on a pitch, so he signaled Shotaro to fire a fastball low to the corner. Shotaro delivered with blazing speed across the outside of the plate, and the batter swung. It one-hopped to Shotaro, who fielded it cleanly in his glove. But as he moved the ball to his open hand he dropped it. The batter made it safely to first.

Come on, man, Nick thought. *Keep it together.*

The other team's pitcher was now up to bat. Like a lot of pitchers, he seemed more hurler than hitter. Nick signed for Shotaro to gun it.

Shotaro wound up and threw, but it was wrong. The pitch came in like a changeup. The Seagulls' pitcher made solid contact and the ball took off. Shotaro looked back over his shoulder in horror and watched the ball fly easily over the fence. About six feet foul.

Nick called for the changeup, but Shotaro sent it so far inside that the batter had to step back from the plate. *Just throw strikes*, Nick willed, but Shotaro couldn't. In no time, the count was 3–1. A pitch later, the other team's pitcher was off to first with a walk. The bases were loaded.

Harris was already on his way to the mound. Nick sprang up and hurried to get to Shotaro first.

"You have to bring it across the plate," Nick said as he reached the mound. "They aren't going to chase if you're not throwing strikes."

"I am throwing 'em," Shotaro said. "Ump's shrunk the strike zone."

Harris was there now. "What's going on, Shotaro?"

"I got this, Coach," Shotaro assured him.

"Nick?" Harris said, looking squarely at him. Nick swallowed. He had already known the answer for the last couple of pitches.

"We need Kurt in," Nick said sadly.

"What?" Shotaro gasped. "You're kidding me! They haven't even scored any runs off me yet!"

"But they will," Nick said, turning away from his friend. "Coach, I think he hurt his arm on that pitch just before bobbling the ball. He's lost the heat."

"Thought so," Harris said. He turned back toward the dugout and signaled for Wash.

"What are you doing?" Shotaro said to Nick. "This is my chance!"

"If you stay in, we're going to lose," Nick answered. "And you'll probably trash your arm for the season. If you're not going to think about the team, think about that."

"You're one to talk," Shotaro said. "You're so intent on getting hits and raising your stats that you're swinging at everything. Who's that helping?"

Once Wash joined the group, he took Shotaro by the elbow with his fingertips.

"Make a fist," he commanded Shotaro. Shotaro obeyed. "Now flex."

As Shotaro began to flex his fist up, Wash pressed with his fingers. Shotaro winced. Wash looked at Harris.

"It's strained all right."

"I can still pitch," Shotaro insisted.

Nick's throat felt thick. He just shook his head.

CHAPTER 15

Sometimes you have to fight fire with fire. Kurt was the Runners' only pitcher with ball movement on par with the Seagulls. Each of their players had dealt with Shotaro's straightforward speed and placement, so now Kurt's slider became a puzzle.

Kurt's first victim managed to foul one off before striking out, and the following batter banged a standard grounder to first. Gus fielded the ball cleanly and whizzed it back to

Nick at home plate, forcing out the run. Nick then returned the favor by throwing out the slower-moving batter still on his way to first for a double play that let the Runners escape with no runs scored.

"Awesome!" Gus yelled, giving Nick a high-five as they left the field.

Shotaro and Wash weren't in the dugout. They were probably at the med station, getting Shotaro checked out. It was probably for the best. The game quickly grew into a pitchers' duel that wouldn't have helped Shotaro's nerves.

Kurt kept batters at bay by allowing only a few hits, few of which resulted in players getting into scoring position before the Roadrunners' defense could close an inning. The Seagulls' pitcher was even more dominant, striking out three of the six batters before Nick came up to bat again with two outs in the top of the fifth.

Despite all that, Nick felt confident. He'd hit this guy once already, almost hitting him for real. Now the pitcher was gun shy. On his first pitch he took some off his follow-through to get ready to defend himself. Nick let it go for a called strike. The ball was moving slower now and breaking earlier.

I can hit this, Nick told himself.

The next pitch was high, but Nick was sure it would break down and away. Nick swung to protect that part of the plate but went under the ball for a strike. This ball had only moved sideways.

I can hit this, Nick repeated.

The next one was outside, and Nick let it break away for a ball.

I can hit this.

Time seemed to slow. The pitcher's arm looked like it was swishing through gel. Nick thought he could see the ball spinning slowly in the air.

I can hit this.

It was the same pitch he'd hit during his last at-bat, breaking in over the middle of the plate. Nick was there. The ball was gone—a blast into left field.

Nick would never be able to put a ball out of this deeper outfield, but the extra field still had its uses. A deeper wall meant widely spaced outfielders with more ground to cover. Neither the left fielder nor the center fielder could reach the hit before it bounced between them and headed deeper out to the fence. Nick was able to slide safely into second untouched.

Holy crap, Nick thought. *Another double!*

A mental copy of his spreadsheet unfolded. Nick was on a great pace for doubles. It was the only stat in which he was outpacing his idols.

Now for some runs, he told himself. But it was unlikely, with two outs and Kurt at bat. Nick watched Kurt take a horrible swing at a ball at his ankles. The Seagulls' pitcher's ball movement bordered on random. It was a wonder the catcher could even track them. Perhaps Nick could use that, though. He took a few steps off second and waited for the windup. His face was calm. It would either work or it wouldn't.

The pitcher kicked. Nick hunched down. The moment the pitcher's arm came forward, Nick ran.

Nick knew the pitcher wouldn't waste pitches on Kurt. He wanted to fan Kurt and end the inning. While slow in his jump for third, Nick's timing was perfect. The catcher saw Nick's attempt to steal and took his eye off the ball long enough to lose it when it curved. Kurt swung and missed completely, and the catcher couldn't get his glove on the ball. It banged off his pads and rolled away.

Kurt scrambled for first as the catcher dove for the ball. Nick was already safe at third when the catcher rose with the ball and fired it to first.

It beat Kurt to the bag by half a second for the third out.

"Nice try," Harris commented as Nick came in. "Almost worked."

"I think we're getting to him, Coach," Nick replied, and moved on to get his gear.

"Nick," Harris said, grabbing his shoulder.

"What?" Nick said nervously.

"If it's still 0–0 and you get on base again, I may have to pull you for a faster runner," Harris said. "Be prepared."

"But I'm having a great game," Nick protested.

"And how many runs has that gotten us?" Harris countered. "You gotta think about the team. Isn't that what you told Shotaro?"

"I think the team stands a better chance of winning with me in the game," Nick said firmly.

"Got some stats to prove that, I suppose?"

Nick shook his head.

"No, sir. Just a gut feeling."

"It's tough to trust the gut completely," Harris said. "There's usually a lot going on in there."

CHAPTER 16

*T*he duel had extended from the pitchers to everyone. The Roadrunners were keeping the Seagulls' players off the base paths with lights-out defense. Kurt rarely struck out anyone, but he and Nick kept the pitches out of each batter's sweet spot. Those that were hit were getting caught, and the balls that didn't get caught were put-outs at first. And none of the very few batters who made it to first ever made it past first.

The Seagulls, on the other hand, had escaped by the skin of their teeth. Their pitcher's movement had dropped off as his pitch count rose, and the Runners were finally hitting onto base. The Roadrunners had gotten two runners on in the sixth but were held off from scoring when Sammy hit into a double play.

"Here we go, Trip," Nick said as Trip went out to start things off in the seventh inning. "We just need one."

Trip had been having a stretch of bad luck. He'd hit two frozen ropes, but fielders in just the right spots had caught both of them.

A pitch came in knee-high for a strike. Trip had the timing down for the next pitch, though, and he clubbed it. The whole bench rose along with the ball. It looked to Nick like the wind was still up there, nudging it even more.

"This one could be gone . . ." said a voice next to Nick. It was Shotaro. Nick hadn't seen him since the second inning. He was wearing an elbow brace wrapped in an ice pack. And he had on his street clothes.

Shotaro seemed neither sad nor angry, but he didn't seem normal either. He seemed far off in his own head. The two watched together in silence as the baseball and the left fielder's glove met at the top of the fence. Trip was out, a few feet shy of a home run.

"How's your arm?" Nick asked Shotaro.

"The EMT looked me over and gave me a brace, but I'll know more when the car shows up to run me over to Flagstaff Medical," Shotaro said. "Feels like crap, though."

"It's good you came out then," Nick said.

Shotaro didn't say anything.

Danny was at the plate now, showing amazing patience as the Seagulls' pitcher struggled to get his pitches over the plate.

"I saw your friend while I was out and about," Shotaro said at last.

Nick raised an eyebrow. "What friend?"

"That scout. He's up on the deck stuffing his face with hot dogs and talking on his cell. Sounds like he's heading out to Seattle tonight."

Nick stiffened. This tournament continued on for two more days.

"Maybe he's seen enough?" Nick said.

Their teammates started clapping. Nick turned. Danny had held tight for a walk. Zack was up to bat. Nick needed to get ondeck.

"Maybe," Shotaro said. "But for now he's still up there."

Nick took a couple of foggy practice swings. *How great would it be to hit another double and drive in the winning run?* he wondered.

Zack fouled away a strike. One and one.

Nick turned his eyes up for a moment toward the party deck Shotaro had mentioned. He couldn't make out anyone clearly from here.

Zack better not hit into a double play. Leading off in the eighth held a lot less opportunity for Nick to shine.

There was a sharp *ping* as Zack hit the ball and took off running. It was a hit to the gap in right. Meanwhile, Danny didn't even consider stopping at second. His incredible speed carried him around to third well in advance of the throw. The outfielder relayed to the second baseman, pinning Zack at first and holding Danny on third.

This is it, Nick realized. *I double here, and I get one . . . maybe two runs batted in. And I'd be on some kind of record pace for doubles. No problem. I own this guy.*

He glanced over to Harris standing outside the dugout. He was signing instructions.

Nick's eyes grew big and his mouth popped open. *That can't be right*, Nick told himself. *Coach is telling me to hit for the fences!*

Harris surely knew, same as Nick, that Nick's odds of knocking a homer were slim to none. What Coach wanted was a sacrifice fly. It felt unnecessary to Nick, maybe even unfair. Nick was a great contact hitter with the ability to find the holes. He'd ended up on second twice tonight already. He knew he could do it again.

"Play ball," the umpire called. Nick approached the plate. He noticed that the middle infielders were playing back and the outfield was playing up. With no force in play at home, the Seagulls were forming a wall that would let them either turn a double play easier or get the ball in to home quickly to hold the runner. Finding a hole would be tough. Perhaps he should go deep like Coach wanted. It might even drop over top.

The pitcher was shaking and nodding at his catcher. The best result for the Seagulls, of course, was to get ahead in the count and strike out Nick. Nick's best chance at a sac fly was right now. The pitcher went to the low inside corner for a strike. Nick's bat never moved.

The wall has a weakness, Nick realized.

The fielder wall was tight and even, but they'd all shifted left, where Nick had been hitting. Too far left. Nick felt sure he could make the adjustment and bat to the opposite field. If he could put it between the first baseman and the right fielder, it might roll straight to the outer corner.

A two-run triple, Nick thought, and readied his bat.

The next pitch was junk, an off-speed pitch too far outside. Nick let it go. The ball was barely breaking at all now.

The next pitch came surprisingly faster, but crashed at the front of the plate for ball two, nearly getting past the catcher. The catcher called time and hurried to the mound. The Seagulls' pitcher was clearly determined to finish the game and was forcing his throws. He was behind in the count now, though. His catcher was probably telling him to calm down and keep it in the strike zone.

His ego's about to cost him this game, Nick thought.

But then another thought hit him.

That last ball still had a lot of movement to it, and speed. There was no guarantee Nick would hit a pitch like that precisely where it would have to go. He thought about the scout in the stands.

I have to try, right? He asked himself. *This might be my last chance to stand out. To show I'm better.*

The catcher had returned to his position at the plate. Nick returned to his too.

Maybe I'll regret it tomorrow, he thought. *But I have to do this thing.*

As Nick had guessed, the pitcher threw a sinking fastball that hung in the strike zone. It was the exactly the pitch Nick wanted. He drilled it.

He dared a glance as he ran toward first. For a second, Nick thought he might actually have hit a home run. The strong breeze was still in play, and the ball he'd launched rose high into the sky. The right fielder had to turn and run as if rabid dogs were at his heels in order to make the catch. After he'd made it, he had no chance of throwing out Danny at home. He could only throw it to second. Zack, who'd stayed near first, gave Nick a high-five as he passed by outside the baseline.

"Good hit, man."

"Thanks," Nick said.

CHAPTER *17*

*I*n the end, the Seagulls' pitcher got his
complete game and an impressive eighth
strikeout by fanning Kurt for the third
out. But he still lost. Kurt had returned the
favor by sitting him down and getting the
remaining two batters to hit into outs. It was
a 1–0 win. The team took the bus to Flagstaff
Medical and sat in the parking lot, where they
watched *Inception* and waited for Shotaro to
finish his exam. Nick was surprised when a

grinning Shotaro muscled past Nick into a nearby seat for the bus ride to the hotel.

"Move over, Man Slut."

Nick grinned. The familiar insult was a good sign.

"Watch those feet, Sho-zilla," Nick responded. He paused for a moment. "You seem upbeat. Good news?"

"Grade 2 UCL strain. Out for four to six weeks probably."

"That doesn't sound like good news . . ." Nick said.

"Well, it could have been a lot worse. Doctor said if I had kept pitching and hadn't iced it down so well, I could have destroyed my tendon."

Shotaro gave his arm a subtle flex and looked it over. "You didn't ruin my chances of getting ahead in baseball after all. You probably saved them."

"So . . . are we cool then?" Nick asked.

"Yeah, of course. You can be a cold, unfeeling, stat-munching robot, but that's what I like about you," Shotaro told him.

"Well, same to you, you hot-headed, self-serving punk," Nick replied.

"At least we figured ourselves out before it really cost us," Shotaro said.

"Our friendship?" Nick asked.

"Winning the game!" Shotaro answered. "Whatever. It all worked out."

Shotaro stared out the window for a moment.

"I suppose I'd never have made it to the seventh inning anyway," Shotaro said.

"Result's the same," Nick said. "A 'no decision.'"

"Oh yeah?" Shotaro challenged with a smile. "I'd have knocked that bum out of the park. I'd have gotten me at least a 2–0 win."

Nick laughed. "Sure you would have."

"I guess a guy's gotta know his limits." Shotaro held up his injured arm for emphasis.

"Tough break today, Mori." Harris had wandered back to join them. "But don't worry. I know the best arm guy in Nevada. You'll be back pitching before you know it."

"Not starting though," Shotaro added.

"Not this year," Harris said. "But you've got promise if you keep at it. Just stay patient for now, okay?" Harris pulled off his cap and scratched through his fuzzy mop of silver hair.

"I'm sure glad that scout's outta here," Harris said. "I think you guys were more interested in him than he was in you."

"How did you know he's gone?" Shotaro said.

"He talked to me a bit after the game," Harris admitted.

Nick couldn't help himself. "What did he say? Was he impressed? What does he think?"

Harris seemed caught off guard. "About you? Nick, he's been tracking Sammy. He never really had any interest in you."

It was like a shot to the gut.

"Why not?"

"Because you don't have the right numbers," Harris explained.

"Which ones?" Nick protested. "Hits? Home runs? Batting average?"

"Height," Harris said bluntly. "This guy doesn't even look at catchers who aren't six feet or taller."

"Are you kidding?" Nick exclaimed. "That's stupid!"

"I agree," Harris said. "Height's only one thing. But then, so is slugging percentage."

Harris scrunched up his face. Getting this deep in a one-on-one with a player wasn't really in his comfort zone. "I'm a straightforward baseball fan. To me, a game only comes down to runs, wins, and losses. Now, I get that the numbers game can be helpful and informative, but there are so many intangibles that are more important."

Nick crossed his arms in silence. He'd driven himself crazy for nothing.

"You had a great game out there Nick, but no stat-tracker would ever know. Certainly not that guy."

. . .

Back at the hotel that night, when everyone was asleep, Nick got his laptop out of his backpack. He was exhausted, but he couldn't sleep yet. He hated leaving things unfinished.

The light from the screen filled the hotel room. Shotaro snored softly from the other bed, his injured arm sandwiched between a pair of pillows.

Nick opened up the spreadsheet he'd been working on the last few weeks. When he'd made it, he'd thought of it as his roadmap to success. Now it looked like nothing more than words and numbers. The widget was still ticking down too.

Nick shut the laptop and lay back down.

I'm more than my numbers. And I'm more than my labels, Nick assured himself, closing his eyes.

ABOUT THE AUTHOR

Jason Glaser is the author of more than 60 nonfiction works for kids, including several books about baseball. His books have appeared on *Booklist*'s "Best of" series awards. He lives in Mankato, Minnesota, and has been a lifelong Twins fan.

"The road to the pros
starts here."

LOOK FOR THESE
TITLES FROM THE

TRAVEL TEAM

COLLECTION.

THE CATCH

When Danny makes "the catch," everyone seems interested in him. Girls text him, kids ask for autographs, and his highlight play even makes it on SportsCenter's Top Plays. A sports-gear executive tempts Danny with a big-money offer, and he decides to take advantage of his newfound fame. Danny agrees to wear the company's gear when he plays. But as his bank account gets bigger, so does his ego. Will Danny be able to keep his head in the game?

POWER HITTER

Sammy Perez has to make it to the big leagues. After his teammate's career-ending injury, the Roadrunners decided to play in a wood bat tournament to protect their pitchers. And while Sammy used to be a hotheaded, hard-hitting, home-run machine, he's now stuck in the slump of his life. Sammy thinks the wood bats are causing the problem, but his dad suggests that maybe he's not strong enough. Is Sammy willing to break the law and sacrifice his health to get an edge by taking performance-enhancing drugs? Can Sammy break out of his slump in time to get noticed by major-league scouts?

FORCED OUT

Zack Waddell's baseball IQ makes him one of the Roadrunners' most important players. When a new kid, Dustin, immediately takes their starting catcher's spot, Zack is puzzled. Dustin doesn't have the skills to be a starter. So Zack offers to help him with his swing in Dustin's swanky personal batting cages.

Zack accidentally overhears a conversation and figures out why Dustin is starting—and why the team is suddenly able to afford an expensive trip to a New York tournament. Will Zack's baseball instincts transfer off the field? Will the Roadrunners be able to stay focused when their team chemistry faces its greatest challenge yet?

THE PROSPECT

Nick Cosimo eats, breathes, and lives baseball. He's a place-hitting catcher, with a cannon for an arm and a calculator for a brain. Thanks to his keen eye, Nick is able to pick apart his opponents, taking advantage of their weaknesses. His teammates and coaches rely on his good instincts between the white lines. But when Nick spots a scout in the stands, everything changes. Will Nick alter his game plan to impress the scout enough to get drafted? Or will Nick put the team before himself?

OUT OF CONTROL

Carlos "Trip" Costas is a fiery shortstop with many talents and passions. His father is Julio Costas—yes, *the* Julio Costas, the famous singer. Unfortunately, Julio is also famous for being loud, controlling, and sometimes violent with Trip. Julio dreams of seeing his son play in the majors, but that's not what Trip wants.

When Trip decides to take a break from baseball to focus on his own music, his father loses his temper. He threatens to stop donating money to the team. Will the Roadrunners survive losing their biggest financial backer and their star shortstop? Will Trip have the courage to follow his dreams and not his father's?

HIGH HEAT

Pitcher Seth Carter had Tommy John surgery on his elbow in hopes of being able to throw harder. Now his fastball cuts through batters like a 90 mph knife through butter. But one day, Seth's pitch gets away from him. The *clunk* of the ball on the batter's skull still haunts Seth in his sleep and on the field. His arm doesn't feel like part of his body anymore, and he goes from being the ace everybody wanted to the pitcher nobody trusts. With the biggest game of the year on the line, can Seth come through for the team?

SOUTHSIDE HIGH

ARE YOU A SURVIVOR?

Check out all the books in the

SURVIVING SOUTH SIDE

collection.

Bad Deal

Fish hates having to take ADHD meds. They help him concentrate but also make him feel weird. So when a cute girl needs a boost to study for tests, Fish offers her one of his pills. Soon more kids want pills, and Fish likes the profits. To keep from running out, Fish finds a doctor who sells phony prescriptions. But suddenly the doctor is arrested. Fish realizes he needs to tell the truth. But will that cost him his friends?

Recruited

Kadeem is a star quarterback for Southside High. He is thrilled when college scouts seek him out. One recruiter even introduces him to a college cheerleader and gives him money to have a good time. But then officials start to investigate illegal recruiting. Will Kadeem decide to help their investigation, even though it means the end of the good times? What will it do to his chances of playing in college?

Benito Runs

Benito's father had been in Iraq for over a year. When he returns, Benito's family life is not the same. Dad suffers from PTSD—post-traumatic stress disorder—and yells constantly. Benito can't handle seeing his dad so crazy, so he decides to run away. Will Benny find a new life? Or will he learn how to deal with his dad—through good times and bad?

Plan B

Lucy has her life planned: She'll graduate and join her boyfriend at college in Austin. She'll become a Spanish teacher, and of course they'll get married. So there's no reason to wait, right? They try to be careful, but Lucy gets pregnant. Lucy's plan is gone. How will she make the most difficult decision of her life?

Beaten

Keah's a cheerleader and Ty's a football star, so they seem like the perfect couple. But when they have their first fight, Ty is beginning to scare Keah with his anger. Then after losing a game, Ty goes ballistic and hits Keah repeatedly. Ty is arrested for assault, but Keah still secretly meets up with Ty. How can Keah be with someone she's afraid of? What's worse—flinching every time your boyfriend gets angry or being alone?

Shattered Star

Cassie is the best singer at Southside and dreams of being famous. She skips school to try out for a national talent competition. But her hopes sink when she sees the line. Then a talent agent shows up, and Cassie is flattered to hear she has "the look" he wants. Soon she is lying and missing rehearsal to meet with him. And he's asking her for more each time. How far will Cassie go for her shot at fame?